Dickory Cronke

By
Daniel Defoe

Dickory Cronke

by Daniel Defoe

ISBN: 978-93-56562-52-3

Published by

DOUBLE 9 BOOKS
2/13-B, Ansari Road
Daryaganj, New Delhi - 110002
info@double9books.com
www.double9books.com
Tel. 011-40042856

This book is under public domain

Printed in India.

About the Author

The English author, writer, artist, and government specialist Daniel Defoe composed in excess of 500 books, flyers, articles, and sonnets. Among the most useful creators of the Augustan Age, he was the first of the extraordinary eighteenth century English writers.

Daniel Defoe was the child of a contradicting London fat chandler or butcher. He early considered turning into a Presbyterian serve, and during the 1670s he went to the Reverend Charles Morton's popular institute close to London. In 1684 he wedded Mary Tuffley, who presented to him the attractive endowment of £3,700. They had seven kids.

Defoe distributed many political and social plots somewhere in the range of 1704 and 1719. During the 1720s he added to such week by week diaries as Mist's and Applebee's, composed criminal accounts, and concentrated on financial matters and geology as well as delivering his significant works of fiction. He passed on in a senseless laziness in Ropemaker's Alley on April 24, 1731, while stowing away from a started bank procedures against him.

Contents

Preface:

The formality of a preface to this little book might have been very well omitted, if it were not to gratify the curiosity of some inquisitive people, who, I foresee, will be apt to make objections against the reality of the narrative. Indeed the public has too often been imposed upon by fictitious stories, and some of a very late date, so that I think myself obliged by the usual respect which is paid to candid and impartial readers, to acquaint them, by way of introduction, with what they are to expect, and what they may depend upon, and yet with this caution too, that it is an indication of ill nature or ill manners, if not both, to pry into a secret that is industriously concealed. However, that there may be nothing wanting on my part, I do hereby assure the reader, that the papers from whence the following sheets were extracted, are now in town, in the custody of a person of unquestionable reputation, who, I will be bold to say, will not only be ready, but proud, to produce them upon a good occasion, and that I think is as much satisfaction as the nature of this case requires. As to the performance, it can signify little now to make an apology upon that account, any farther than this, that if the reader pleases he may take notice that what he has now before him was collected from a large bundle of papers, most of which were writ in shorthand, and very ill-digested. However, this may be relied upon, that though the language is something altered, and now and then a word thrown in to help the expression, yet strict care has been taken to speak the author's mind, and keep as close as possible to the meaning of the original. For the design, I think there is nothing need be said in vindication of that. Here is a dumb philosopher introduced to a wicked and degenerate generation, as a proper emblem of virtue and morality; and if the world could be persuaded to look upon him with candour and impartiality, and then to copy after him, the editor has gained his end, and would think himself sufficiently recompensed for his present trouble.

Part I:

Among the many strange and surprising events that help to fill the accounts of this last century, I know none that merit more an entire credit, or are more fit to be preserved and handed to posterity than those I am now going to lay before the public.

Dickory Cronke, the subject of the following narrative, was born at a little hamlet, near St. Columb, in Cornwall, on the 29th of May, 1660, being the day and year in which King Charles the Second was restored. His parents were of mean extraction, but honest, industrious people, and well beloved in their neighbourhood. His father's chief business was to work at the tin mines; his mother stayed at home to look after the children, of which they had several living at the same time. Our Dickory was the youngest, and being but a sickly child, had always a double portion of her care and tenderness.

It was upwards of three years before it was discovered that he was born dumb, the knowledge of which at first gave his mother great uneasiness, but finding soon after that he had his hearing, and all his other senses to the greatest perfection, her grief began to abate, and she resolved to have him brought up as well as their circumstances and his capacity would permit.

As he grew, notwithstanding his want of speech, he every day gave some instance of a ready genius, and a genius much superior to the country children, insomuch that several gentlemen in the neighbourhood took particular notice of him, and would often call him Restoration Dick, and give him money, &c.

When he came to be eight years of age, his mother agreed with a person in the next village, to teach him to read and write, both which, in a very short time, he acquired to such perfection, especially the latter, that he not only taught his own brothers and sisters, but likewise several young men and women in the neighbourhood, which often brought him in small sums, which he always laid out in such necessaries as he stood most in need of.

In this state he continued till he was about twenty, and then he began to reflect how scandalous it was for a young man of his age and circumstances to live idle at home, and so resolves to go with his father to the mines, to try if he could get something towards the support of himself and the family; but being of a tender constitution, and often sick, he soon perceived that sort of business was too hard for him, so was forced to return home and continue in his former station; upon which he grew exceeding melancholy, which his mother observing, she comforted him in the best manner she could, telling him that if it should please God to take her away, she had something left in store for him, which would preserve him against public want.

This kind assurance from a mother whom he so dearly loved gave him some, though not an entire satisfaction; however, he resolves to acquiesce under it till Providence should order something for him more to his content and advantage, which, in a short time happened according to his wish. The manner was thus:-

One Mr. Owen Parry, a Welsh gentleman of good repute, coming from Bristol to Padstow, a little seaport in the county of Cornwall, near the place where Dickory dwelt, and hearing much of this dumb man's perfections, would needs have him sent for; and finding, by his significant gestures and all outward appearances that he much exceeded the character that the country gave of him, took a mighty liking to him, insomuch that he told him, if he would go with him into Pembrokeshire, he would be kind to him, and take care of him as long as he lived.

This kind and unexpected offer was so welcome to poor Dickory, that without any farther consideration, he got a pen and ink and writ a note, and in a very handsome and submissive manner returned him thanks for his favour, assuring him he would do his best to continue and improve it; and that he would be ready to wait upon him whenever he should be pleased to command.

To shorten the account as much as possible, all things were concluded to their mutual satisfaction, and in about a fortnight's time they set forward for Wales, where Dickory, notwithstanding his dumbness, behaved himself with so much diligence and affability, that he not only gained the love of the family where he lived, but of everybody round him.

In this station he continued till the death of his master, which happened about twenty years afterwards; in all which time, as has been confirmed by several of the family, he was never observed to be any ways disguised by drinking, or to be guilty of any of the follies and irregularities incident to servants in gentlemen's houses. On the contrary, when he had any spare time, his constant custom was to retire with some good book into a private place within call, and there employ himself in reading, and then writing down his observations upon what he read.

After the death of his master, whose loss afflicted him to the last degree, one Mrs. Mary Mordant, a gentlewoman of great virtue and piety, and a very good fortune, took him into her service, and carried him with her, first to Bath, and then to Bristol, where, after a lingering distemper, which continued for about four years, she died likewise.

Upon the loss of his mistress, Dickory grew again exceeding melancholy and disconsolate; at length, reflecting that death is but a common debt which all mortals owe to nature, and must be paid sooner or later, he became a little better satisfied, and so determines to get together what he had saved in his service, and then to return to his native country, and there finish his life in privacy and retirement.

Having been, as has been mentioned, about twenty-four years a servant, and having, in the interim, received two legacies, viz., one of thirty pounds, left him by his master, and another of fifteen pounds by his mistress, and being always very frugal, he had got by him in the whole upwards of sixty pounds. This, thinks he, with prudent management, will be enough to support me as long as I live, and so I'll e'en lay aside all thoughts of future business, and make the best of my way to Cornwall, and there find out some safe and solitary retreat, where I may have liberty to meditate and make my melancholy observations upon the several occurrences of human life.

This resolution prevailed so far, that no time was let slip to get everything in readiness to go with the first ship. As to his money, he always kept that locked up by him, unless he sometimes lent it to a friend without interest, for he had a mortal hatred to all sorts of usury or extortion. His books, of which he had a considerable quantity, and some of them very good ones, together with his other equipage, he got packed up, that nothing might be wanting against the first opportunity.

In a few days he heard of a vessel bound to Padstow, the very port he wished to go to, being within four or five miles of the place where he was born. When he came thither, which was in less than a week, his first business was to inquire after the state of his family. It was some time before he could get any information of them, until an old man that knew his father and mother, and remembered they had a son was born dumb, recollected him, and after a great deal of difficulty, made him understand that all his family except his youngest sister were dead, and that she was a widow, and lived at a little town called St. Helen's, about ten miles farther in the country.

This doleful news, we must imagine, must be extremely shocking, and add a new sting to his former affliction; and here it was that he began to exercise the philosopher, and to demonstrate himself both a wise and a good man. All these things, thinks he, are the will of Providence, and must not be disputed; and so he bore up under them with an entire resignation, resolving that, as soon as he could find a place where he might deposit his trunk and boxes with safety, he would go to St. Helen's in quest of his sister.

How his sister and he met, and how transported they were to see each other after so long an interval, I think is not very material. It is enough for the present purpose that Dickory soon recollected his sister, and she him; and after a great many endearing tokens of love and tenderness, he wrote to her, telling her that he believed Providence had bestowed on him as much as would support him as long as he lived, and that if she thought proper he would come and spend the remainder of his days with her.

The good woman no sooner read his proposal than she accepted it, adding, withal, that she could wish her entertainment was better; but if he would accept of it as it was, she would do her best to make everything easy, and that he should be welcome upon his own terms, to stay with her as long as he pleased.

This affair being so happily settled to his full satisfaction, he returns to Padstow to fetch the things he had left behind him, and the next day came back to St. Helen's, where, according to his own proposal, he continued to the day of his death, which happened upon the 29th of May, 1718, about the same hour in which he was born.

Having thus given a short detail of the several periods of his life, extracted chiefly from the papers which he left behind him, I come in the next place to make a few observations how he managed himself and spent his time toward the latter part of it.

His constant practice, both winter and summer, was to rise and set with the sun; and if the weather would permit, he never failed to walk in some unfrequented place, for three hours, both morning and evening, and there it is supposed he composed the following meditations. The chief part of his sustenance was milk, with a little bread boiled in it, of which in the morning, after his walk, he would eat the quantity of a pint, and sometimes more. Dinners he never eat any; and at night he would only have a pretty large piece of bread, and drink a draught of good spring water; and after this method he lived during the whole time he was at St. Helen's. It is observed of him that he never slept out of a bed, nor never lay awake in one; which I take to be an argument, not only of a strong and healthful constitution, but of a mind composed and calm, and entirely free from the ordinary disturbances of human life. He never gave the least signs of complaint or dissatisfaction at anything, unless it was when he heard the tinners swear, or saw them drunk; and then, too, he would get out of the way as soon as he had let them see, by some significant signs, how scandalous and ridiculous they made themselves; and against the next time he met them, would be sure to have a paper ready written, wherein he would represent the folly of drunkenness, and the dangerous consequences that generally attended it.

Idleness was his utter aversion, and if at any time he had finished the business of the day, and was grown weary of reading and writing, in which he daily spent six hours at least, he would certainly find something either within doors or without, to employ himself.

Much might be said both with regard to the wise and regular management, and the prudent methods he took to spend his time well towards the declension of his life; but, as his history may perhaps be shortly published at large by a better hand, I shall only observe in the general, that he was a person of great wisdom and sagacity. He understood nature beyond the ordinary capacity, and, if he had had a competency of learning suitable to his genius, neither this nor the former ages would have produced a better philosopher or a greater man.

I come next to speak of the manner of his death and the consequences thereof, which are, indeed, very surprising, and, perhaps, not altogether unworthy a general observation. I shall relate them as briefly as I can, and leave every one to believe or disbelieve as he thinks proper.

Upon the 26th of May, 1718, according to his usual method, about four in the afternoon, he went out to take his evening walk; but before he could reach the place he intended, he was siezed with an apoplectic fit, which only gave him liberty to sit down under a tree, where, in an instant, he was deprived of all manner of sense and motion, and so he continued, as appears by his own confession afterwards, for more than fourteen hours.

His sister, who knew how exact he was in all his methods, finding him stay a considerable time beyond the usual hour, concludes that some misfortune must needs have happened to him, or he would certainly have been at home before. In short, she went immediately to all the places he was wont to frequent, but nothing could be heard or seen of him till the next morning, when a young man, as he was going to work, discovered him, and went home and told his sister that her brother lay in such a place, under a tree, and, as he believed had been robbed and murdered.

The poor woman, who had all night been under the most dreadful apprehensions, was now frightened and confounded to the last degree. However, recollecting herself, and finding there was no remedy, she got two or three of her neighbours to bear her company, and so hastened with the young man to the tree, where she found her brother lying in the same posture that he had described.

The dismal object at first view startled and surprised everybody present, and filled them full of different notions and conjectures. But some of the company going nearer to him, and finding that he had lost nothing, and that there were no marks of any violence to be discovered about him, they conclude that it must be an apoplectic or some other sudden fit that had surprised him in his walk, upon which his sister and the rest began to feel his hands and face, and observing that he was still warm, and that there were some symptoms of life yet remaining, they conclude that the best way was to carry him home to bed, which was accordingly done with the utmost expedition.

When they had got him into the bed, nothing was omitted that they could think of to bring him to himself, but still he continued utterly insensible for about six hours. At the sixth hour's end he began to move a little, and in a very short time was so far recovered, to the great astonishment of everybody about him, that he was able to look up, and to make a sign to his sister to bring him a cup of water.

After he had drunk the water he soon perceived that all his faculties were returned to their former stations, and though his strength was very much abated by the length and rigour of the fit, yet his intellects were as strong and vigorous as ever.

His sister observing him to look earnestly upon the company, as if he had something extraordinary to communicate to them, fetched him a pen and ink and a sheet of paper, which, after a short pause, he took, and wrote as follows:-

"Dear sister,

"I have now no need of pen, ink, and paper, to tell you my meaning. I find the strings that bound up my tongue, and hindered me from speaking, are unloosed, and I have words to express myself as freely and distinctly as any other person. From whence this strange and unexpected event should proceed, I must not pretend to say, any farther than this, that it is doubtless the hand of Providence that has done it, and in that I ought to acquiesce. Pray let me be alone for two or three hours, that I may be at liberty to compose myself, and put my thoughts in the best order I can before I leave them behind me."

The poor woman, though extremely startled at what her brother had written, yet took care to conceal it from the neighbours, who, she knew, as well as she, must be mightily surprised at a thing so utterly unexpected. Says she, my brother desires to be alone; I believe he may have something in his mind that disturbs him. Upon which the neighbours took their leave and returned home, and his sister shut the door, and left him alone to his private contemplations.

After the company were withdrawn he fell into a sound sleep, which lasted from two till six, and his sister, being apprehensive of the return of his fit, came to the bedside, and, asking softly if he wanted anything, he turned about to her and spoke to this effect:

Dear sister, you see me not only recovered out of a terrible fit, but likewise that I have the liberty of speech, a blessing that I have been deprived of almost sixty years, and I am satisfied you are sincerely joyful to find me in the state I now am in; but, alas! it is but a mistaken kindness. These are things but of short duration, and if they were to continue for a hundred years longer, I can't see how I should be anyways the better.

I know the world too well to be fond of it, and am fully satisfied that the difference between a long and a short life is insignificant, especially when I consider the accidents and company I am to encounter. Do but look seriously and impartially upon the astonishing notion of time and eternity, what an immense deal has run out already, and how infinite it is still in the future; do but seriously and deliberately consider this, and you will find, upon the whole, that three days and three ages of life come much to the same measure and reckoning.

As soon as he had ended his discourse upon the vanity and uncertainty of human life, he looked steadfastly upon her. Sister, says he, I conjure you not to be disturbed at what I am going to tell you, which you will undoubtedly find to be true in every particular. I perceive my glass is run, and I have now no more to do in this world but to take my leave of it; for to-morrow about this time my speech will be again taken from me, and, in a short time, my fit will return; and the next day, which I understand is the day on which I came into this troublesome world, I shall exchange it for another, where, for the future, I shall for ever be free from all manner of sin and sufferings.

The good woman would have made him a reply, but he prevented her by telling her he had no time to hearken to unnecessary complaints or animadversions. I have a great many things in my mind, says he, that require a speedy and serious consideration. The time I have to stay is but short, and I have a great deal of important business to do in it. Time and death are both in my view, and seem both to call aloud to me to make no delay. I beg of you, therefore, not to disquiet yourself or me. What must be, must be. The decrees of Providence are eternal and unalterable; why, then, should we torment ourselves about that which we cannot remedy?

I must confess, my dear sister, I owe you many obligations for your exemplary fondness to me, and do solemnly assure you I shall retain the sense of them to the last moment. All that I have to request of you is, that I may be alone for this night. I have it in my thoughts to leave some short observations behind me, and likewise to discover some things of great weight which have been revealed to me, which may perhaps be of some use hereafter to you and your friends. What credit they may meet with I cannot say, but depend the consequence, according to their respective periods, will account for them, and vindicate them against the supposition of falsity and mere suggestion.

Upon this, his sister left him till about four in the morning, when coming to his bedside to know if he wanted anything, and how he had rested, he made her this answer; I have been taking a cursory view of my life, and though I find myself exceedingly deficient in several particulars, yet I bless God I cannot find I have any just grounds to suspect my pardon. In short, says he, I have spent this night with more inward pleasure and true satisfaction than ever I spent a night through the whole course of my life.

After he had concluded what he had to say upon the satisfaction that attended an innocent and well-spent life, and observed what a mighty consolation it was to persons, not only under the apprehension, but even in the very agonies of death itself, he desired her to bring him his usual cup of water, and then to help him on with his clothes, that he might sit up, and so be in a better posture to take his leave of her and her friends.

When she had taken him up, and placed him at a table where he usually sat, he desired her to bring him his box of papers, and after he had collected those he intended should be preserved, he ordered her to bring a candle, that he might see the rest burnt. The good woman seemed at first to oppose the burning of his papers, till he told her they were only useless trifles, some unfinished observations which he had made in his youthful days, and were not fit to be seen by her, or anybody that should come after him.

After he had seen his papers burnt, and placed the rest in their proper order, and had likewise settled all his other affairs, which was only fit to be done between himself and his sister, he desired her to call two or three of the most reputable neighbours, not only to be witnesses of his will, but likewise to hear what he had farther to communicate before the return of his fit, which he expected very speedily.

His sister, who had beforehand acquainted two or three of her confidants with all that had happened, was very much rejoiced to hear her brother make so unexpected a concession; and accordingly, without any delay or hesitation, went directly into the neighbourhood, and brought home her two select friends, upon whose secrecy and sincerity she knew she might depend upon all accounts.

In her absence he felt several symptoms of the approach of his fit, which made him a little uneasy, lest it should entirely seize him before he had perfected his will, but that apprehension was quickly removed by her speedy return. After she had introduced her friends into his chamber, he proceeded to express himself in the following manner; Dear sister, you now see your brother upon the brink of eternity; and as the words of dying persons are commonly the most regarded, and make deepest impressions, I cannot suspect but you will suffer the few I am about to say to have always some place in your thoughts, that they may be ready for you to make use of upon any occasion.

Do not be fond of anything on this side of eternity, or suffer your interest to incline you to break your word, quit your modesty, or to do anything that will not bear the light, and look the world in the face. For be assured of this; the person that values the virtue of his mind and the dignity of his reason, is always easy and well fortified both against death and misfortune, and is perfectly indifferent about the length or shortness of his life. Such a one is solicitous about nothing but his own conduct, and for fear he should be deficient in the duties of religion, and the respective functions of reason and prudence.

Always go the nearest way to work. Now, the nearest way through all the business of human life, are the paths of religion and honesty, and keeping those as directly as you can, you avoid all the dangerous precipices that often lie in the road, and sometimes block up the passage entirely.

Remember that life was but lent at first, and that the remainder is more than you have reason to expect, and consequently ought to be managed with more than ordinary diligence. A wise man spends every day as if it were his last; his hourglass is always in his hand, and he is never guilty of sluggishness or insincerity.

He was about to proceed, when a sudden symptom of the return of his fit put him in mind that it was time to get his will witnessed, which was no sooner done but he took it up and gave it to his sister, telling her that though all he had was hers of right, yet he thought it proper, to prevent even a possibility of a dispute, to write down his mind in the nature of a will, wherein I have given you, says he, the little that I have left, except my books and papers, which, as soon as I am dead, I desire may be delivered to Mr. Anthony Barlow, a near relation of my worthy master, Mr. Owen Parry.

This Mr. Anthony Barlow was an old contemplative Welsh gentleman, who, being under some difficulties in his own country, was forced to come into Cornwall and take sanctuary among the tinners. Dickory, though he kept himself as retired as possible, happened to meet him one day upon his walks, and presently remembered that he was the very person that used frequently to come to visit his master while he lived in Pembrokeshire, and so went to him, and by signs made him understand who he was.

The old gentleman, though at first surprised at this unexpected interview, soon recollected that he had formerly seen at Mr. Parry's a dumb man, whom they used to call the dumb philosopher, so concludes immediately that consequently this must be he. In short, they soon made themselves known to each other; and from that time contracted a strict friendship and a correspondence by letters, which for the future they mutually managed with the greatest exactness and familiarity.

But to leave this as a matter not much material, and to return to our narrative. By this time Dickory's speech began to falter, which his sister observing, put him in mind that he would do well to make some declaration of his faith and principles of religion, because some reflections had been made upon him upon the account of his neglect, or rather his refusal, to appear at any place of public worship.

"Dear sister," says he, "you observe very well, and I wish the continuance of my speech for a few moments, that I might make an ample declaration upon that account. But I find that cannot be; my speech is leaving me so fast that I can only tell you that I have always lived, and now die, an unworthy member of the ancient catholic and apostolic church; and as to my faith and principles, I refer you to my papers, which, I hope, will in some measure vindicate me against the reflections you mention."

He had hardly finished his discourse to his sister and her two friends, and given some short directions relating to his burial, but his speech left him; and what makes the thing the more remarkable, it went away, in all appearance, without giving him any sort of pain or uneasiness.

When he perceived that his speech was entirely vanished, and that he was again in his original state of dumbness, he took his pen as formerly and wrote to his sister, signifying that whereas the sudden loss of his speech had deprived him of the opportunity to speak to her and her friends what he intended, he would leave it for them in writing, and so desired he might not be disturbed till the return of his fit, which he expected in six hours at farthest. According to his desire they all left him, and then, with the greatest resignation imaginable, he wrote down the meditations following:

Part II

An Abstract of his Faith, and the Principles of his Religion &c., which begins thus:

Dear Sister; I thank you for putting me in mind to make a declaration of my faith, and the principles of my religion. I find, as you very well observe, I have been under some reflections upon that account, and therefore I think it highly requisite that I set that matter right in the first place. To begin, therefore, with my faith, in which I intend to be as short and as comprehensive as I can:

1. I most firmly believe that it was the eternal will of God, and the result of his infinite wisdom, to create a world, and for the glory of his majesty to make several sorts of creatures in order and degree one after another; that is to say, angels, or pure immortal spirits; men, consisting of immortal spirits and matter, having rational and sensitive souls; brutes, having mortal and sensitive souls; and mere vegetatives, such as trees, plants, &c.; and these creatures so made do, as it were, clasp the higher and lower world together.

2. I believe the holy Scriptures, and everything therein contained, to be the pure and essential word of God; and that, according to these sacred writings, man, the lord and prince of the creation, by his disobedience in Paradise, forfeited his innocence and the dignity of his nature, and subjected himself and all his posterity to sin and misery.

3. I believe and am fully and entirely satisfied, that God the Father, out of his infinite goodness and compassion to mankind, was pleased to send his only Son, the second person in the holy and undivided Trinity, to meditate for him, and to procure his redemption and eternal salvation.

4. I believe that God the Son, out of his infinite love, and for the glory of the Deity, was pleased voluntarily and freely to descend from

heaven, and to take our nature upon him, and to lead an exemplary life of purity, holiness, and perfect obedience, and at last to suffer an ignominious death upon the cross, for the sins of the whole world, and to rise again the third day for our justification.

5. I believe that the Holy Ghost out of his infinite goodness was pleased to undertake the office of sanctifying us with his divine grace, and thereby assisting us with faith to believe, will to desire, and power to do all those things that are required of us in this world, in order to entitle us to the blessings of just men made perfect in the world to come.

6. I believe that these three persons are of equal power, majesty, and duration, and that the Godhead of the Father, of the Son, and of the Holy Ghost is all one, and that they are equally uncreate, incomprehensible, eternal, and almighty; and that none is greater or less than the other, but that every one hath one and the same divine nature and perfections.

These, sister, are the doctrines which have been received and practised by the best men of every age, from the beginning of the Christian religion to this day, and it is upon this I ground my faith and hopes of salvation, not doubting but, if my life and practice have been answerable to them, that I shall be quickly translated out of this kingdom of darkness, out of this world of sorrow, vexation and confusion, into that blessed kingdom, where I shall cease to grieve and to suffer, and shall be happy to all eternity.

As to my principles in religion, to be as brief as I can, I declare myself to be a member of Christ's church, which I take to be a universal society of all Christian people, distributed under lawful governors and pastors into particular churches, holding communion with each other in all the essentials of the Christian faith, worship, and discipline; and among these I look upon the Church of England to be the chief and best constituted.

The Church of England is doubtless the great bulwark of the ancient Catholic or Apostolic faith all over the world; a church that has all the spiritual advantages that the nature of a church is capable of. From the doctrine and principles of the Church of England, we are taught loyalty to our prince, fidelity to our country, and justice to all mankind; and therefore, as I look upon this to be one of the most excellent branches of the Church Universal, and stands, as it were, between superstition and hypocrisy, I therefore declare, for the satisfaction of you and your friends, as I have always lived so I now die, a true and sincere, though a most unworthy member of it. And as to my discontinuance of my attendance at the public worship, I refer you to my papers, which I have left with my worthy friend, Mr. Barlow. And thus, my dear sister, I have given you a short account of my faith, and the principles of my religion. I come, in the next place, to lay before you a few meditations and observations I have at several times collected together, more particularly those since my retirement to St. Helen's.

Meditations and Observations relating to the Conduct of Human Life in general.

1. Remember how often you have neglected the great duties of religion and virtue, and slighted the opportunities that Providence has put into your hands; and, withal, that you have a set period assigned you for the management of the affairs of human life; and then reflect seriously that, unless you resolve immediately to improve the little remains, the whole must necessarily slip away insensibly, and then you are lost beyond recovery.

2. Let an unaffected gravity, freedom, justice, and sincerity shine through all your actions, and let no fancies and chimeras give the least check to those excellent qualities. This is an easy task, if you will but suppose everything you do to be your last, and if you can keep your passions and appetites from crossing your reason. Stand clear of rashness, and have nothing of insincerity or self-love to infect you.

3. Manage all your thoughts and actions with such prudence and circumspection as if you were sensible you were just going to step into the grave. A little thinking will show a man the vanity and uncertainty of all sublunary things, and enable him to examine maturely the manner of dying; which, if duly abstracted from the terror of the idea, will appear nothing more than an unavoidable appendix of life itself, and a pure natural action.

4. Consider that ill-usage from some sort of people is in a manner necessary, and therefore do not be disquieted about it, but rather conclude that you and your enemy are both marching off the stage together, and that in a little time your very memories will be extinguished.

5. Among your principal observations upon human life, let it be always one to take notice what a great deal both of time and ease that man gains who is not troubled with the spirit of curiosity, who lets his neighbours' affairs alone, and confines his inspections to himself, and only takes care of honesty and a good conscience.

6. If you would live at your ease, and as much as possible be free from the incumbrances of life, manage but a few things at once, and let those, too, be such as are absolutely necessary. By this rule you will draw the bulk of your business into a narrow compass, and have the double pleasure of making your actions good, and few into the bargain.

7. He that torments himself because things do not happen just as he would have them, is but a sort of ulcer in the world; and he that is selfish, narrow-souled, and sets up for a separate interest, is a kind of voluntary outlaw, and disincorporates himself from mankind.

8. Never think anything below you which reason and your own circumstances require, and never suffer yourself to be deterred by the ill-grounded notions of censure and reproach; but when honesty and conscience prompt you to say or do anything, do it boldly; never balk your resolution or start at the consequence.

9. If a man does me an injury, what is that to me? It is his own action, and let him account for it. As for me, I am in my proper station, and only doing the business that Providence has allotted; and withal, I ought to consider that the best way to revenge, is not to imitate the injury.

10. When you happen to be ruffled and put out of humour by any cross accident, retire immediately into your reason, and do not suffer your passion to overrule you a moment; for the sooner you recover yourself now, the better you will be able to guard yourself for the future.

11. Do not be like those ill-natured people that, though they do not love to give a good word to their contemporaries, yet are mighty fond of their own commendations. This argues a perverse and unjust temper, and often exposes the authors to scorn and contempt.

12. If any one convinces you of an error, change your opinion and thank him for it: truth and information are your business, and can

never hurt anybody. On the contrary, he that is proud and stubborn, and wilfully continues in a mistake, it is he that receives the mischief.

13. Because you see a thing difficult, do not instantly conclude it to be impossible to master it. Diligence and industry are seldom defeated. Look, therefore, narrowly into the thing itself, and what you observe proper and practicable in another, conclude likewise within your own power.

14. The principal business of human life is run through within the short compass of twenty-four hours; and when you have taken a deliberate view of the present age, you have seen as much as if you had begun with the world, the rest being nothing else but an endless round of the same thing over and over again.

15. Bring your will to your fate, and suit your mind to your circumstances. Love your friends and forgive your enemies, and do justice to all mankind, and you will be secure to make your passage easy, and enjoy most of the comforts human life is capable to afford you.

16. When you have a mind to entertain yourself in your retirements, let it be with the good qualifications of your friends and acquaintance. Think with pleasure and satisfaction upon the honour and bravery of one, the modesty of another, the generosity of a third, and so on; there being nothing more pleasant and diverting than the lively images and the advantages of those we love and converse with.

17. As nothing can deprive you of the privileges of your nature, or compel you to act counter to your reason, so nothing can happen to you but what comes from Providence, and consists with the interest of the universe.

18. Let people's tongues and actions be what they will, your business is to have honour and honesty in your view. Let them rail, revile, censure, and condemn, or make you the subject of their scorn and ridicule, what does it all signify? You have one certain remedy against all their malice and folly, and that is, to live so that nobody shall believe them.

19. Alas, poor mortals! did we rightly consider our own state and condition, we should find it would not be long before we have forgot all the world, and to be even, that all the world will have forgot us likewise.

20. He that would recommend himself to the public, let him do it by the candour and modesty of his behaviour, and by a generous indifference to external advantages. Let him love mankind, and resign to Providence, and then his works will follow him, and his good actions will praise him in the gate.

21. When you hear a discourse, let your understanding, as far as possible, keep pace with it, and lead you forward to those things which fall most within the compass of your own observations.

22. When vice and treachery shall be rewarded, and virtue and ability slighted and discountenanced; when ministers of state shall rather fear man than God, and to screen themselves run into parties and factions; when noise and clamour, and scandalous reports shall carry everything before them, it is natural to conclude that a nation in such a state of infatuation stands upon the brink of destruction, and without the intervention of some unforeseen accident, must be inevitably ruined.

23. When a prince is guarded by wise and honest men, and when all public officers are sure to be rewarded if they do well, and punished if they do evil, the consequence is plain; justice and honesty will flourish, and men will be always contriving, not for themselves, but for the honour and interest of their king and country.

24. Wicked men may sometimes go unpunished in this world, but wicked nations never do; because this world is the only place of punishment of wicked nations, though not for private and particular persons.

25. An administration that is merely founded upon human policy must be always subject to human chance; but that which is founded on the divine wisdom can no more miscarry than the government of heaven. To govern by parties and factions is the advice of an atheist, and sets up a government by the spirit of Satan. In such a government the prince can never be secure under the greatest promises, since, as men's interest changes, so will their duty and affections likewise.

26. It is a very ancient observation, and a very true one, that people generally despise where they flatter, and cringe to those they design to betray; so that truth and ceremony are, and always will be, two distinct things.

27. When you find your friend in an error, undeceive him with secrecy and civility, and let him see his oversight first by hints and glances; and if you cannot convince him, leave him with respect, and lay the fault upon your own management.

28. When you are under the greatest vexations, then consider that human life lasts but for a moment; and do not forget but that you are like the rest of the world, and faulty yourself in many instances; and withal, remember that anger and impatience often prove more mischievous than the provocation.

29. Gentleness and good humour are invincible, provided they are without hypocrisy and design; they disarm the most barbarous and savage tempers, and make even malice ashamed of itself.

30. In all the actions of life let it be your first and principal care to guard against anger on the one hand, and flattery on the other, for they are both unserviceable qualities, and do a great deal of mischief in the government of human life.

31. When a man turns knave or libertine, and gives way to fear, jealousy, and fits of the spleen; when his mind complains of his fortune, and he quits the station in which Providence has placed him, he acts perfectly counter to humanity, deserts his own nature, and, as it were, runs away from himself.

32. Be not heavy in business, disturbed in conversation, nor impertinent in your thoughts. Let your judgment be right, your actions friendly, and your mind contented; let them curse you, threaten you, or despise you; let them go on; they can never injure your reason or your virtue, and then all the rest that they can do to you signifies nothing.

33. The only pleasure of human life is doing the business of the creation; and which way is that to be compassed very easily? Most certainly by the practice of general kindness, by rejecting the importunity of our senses, by distinguishing truth from falsehood, and by contemplating the works of the Almighty.

34. Be sure to mind that which lies before you, whether it be thought, word, or action; and never postpone an opportunity, or make virtue wait for you till to-morrow.

35. Whatever tends neither to the improvement of your reason nor the benefit of society, think it below you; and when you have

done any considerable service to mankind, do not lessen it by your folly in gaping after reputation and requital.

36. When you find yourself sleepy in a morning, rouse yourself, and consider that you are born to business, and that in doing good in your generation, you answer your character and act like a man; whereas sleep and idleness do but degrade you, and sink you down to a brute.

37. A mind that has nothing of hope, or fear, or aversion, or desire, to weaken and disturb it, is the most impregnable security. Hither we may with safety retire and defy our enemies; and he that sees not this advantage must be extremely ignorant, and he that forgets it unhappy.

38. Do not disturb yourself about the faults of other people, but let everybody's crimes be at their own door. Have always this great maxim in your remembrance, that to play the knave is to rebel against religion; all sorts of injustice being no less than high treason against Heaven itself.

39. Do not contemn death, but meet it with a decent and religious fortitude, and look upon it as one of those things which Providence has ordered. If you want a cordial to make the apprehensions of dying go down a little the more easily, consider what sort of world and what sort of company you will part with. To conclude, do but look seriously into the world, and there you will see multitudes of people preparing for funerals, and mourning for their friends and acquaintances; and look out again a little afterwards, and you will see others doing the very same thing for them.

40. In short, men are but poor transitory things. To-day they are busy and harassed with the affairs of human life; and to-morrow life itself is taken from them, and they are returned to their original dust and ashes. Part III:

Containing prophetic observations relating to the affairs of Europe and of Great Britain, more particularly from 1720 to 1729.

1. In the latter end of 1720, an eminent old lady shall bring forth five sons at a birth; the youngest shall live and grow up to maturity, but the four eldest shall either die in the nursery, or be all carried off by one sudden and unexpected accident.

2. About this time a man with a double head shall arrive in Britain from the south. One of these heads shall deliver messages of great importance to the governing party, and the other to the party that is opposite to them. The first shall believe the monster, but the last shall discover the impostor, and so happily disengage themselves from a snare that was laid to destroy them and their posterity. After this the two heads shall unite, and the monster shall appear in his proper shape.

3. In the year 1721, a philosopher from Lower Germany shall come, first to Amsterdam in Holland, and afterwards to London. He will bring with him a world of curiosities, and among them a pretended secret for the transmutation of metals. Under the umbrage of this mighty secret he shall pass upon the world for some time; but at length he shall be detected, and proved to be nothing but an empiric and a cheat, and so forced to sneak off, and leave the people he has deluded, either to bemoan their loss, or laugh at their own folly. N.B.- This will be the last of his sect that will ever venture in this part of the world upon the same errand.

4. In this year great endeavours will be used for procuring a general peace, which shall be so near a conclusion that public rejoicings shall be made at the courts of several great potentates upon that account; but just in the critical juncture, a certain neighbouring prince shall come to a violent death, which shall occasion new war and commotion all over Europe; but these shall continue but for a short time, and at last terminate in the utter destruction of the first aggressors.

5. Towards the close of this year of mysteries, a person that was born blind shall have his sight restored, and shall see ravens perch upon the heads of traitors, among which the head of a notorious prelate shall stand upon the highest pole.

6. In the year 1722, there shall be a grand congress, and new overtures of peace offered by most of the principal parties concerned in the war, which shall have so good effect that a cessation of arms shall be agreed upon for six months, which shall be kept inviolable till a certain general, either through treachery or inadvertency, shall begin hostilities before the expiration of the term; upon which the injured prince shall draw his sword, and throw the scabbard into

Dickory Cronke

the sea, vowing never to return it till he shall obtain satisfaction for himself, and done justice to all that were oppressed.

7. At the close of this year, a famous bridge shall be broken down, and the water that runs under it shall be tinctured with the blood of two notorious malefactors, whose unexpected death shall make mighty alterations in the present state of affairs, and put a stop to the ruin of a nation, which must otherwise have been unavoidable.

8. 1723 begins with plots, conspiracies, and intestine commotions in several countries; nor shall Great Britain itself be free from the calamity. These shall continue till a certain young prince shall take the reins of government into his own hands; and after that, a marriage shall be proposed, and an alliance concluded between two great potentates, who shall join their forces, and endeavour, in good earnest, to set all matters upon a right foundation.

9. This year several cardinals and prelates shall be publicly censured for heretical principles, and shall narrowly escape from being torn to pieces by the common people, who still look upon them as the grand disturbers of public tranquillity, perfect incendiaries, and the chief promoters of their former, present, and future calamities.

10. In 1724-5 there will be many treaties and negociations, and Great Britain, particularly, will be crowded with foreign ministers and ambassadors from remote princes and states. Trade and commerce will begin to flourish and revive, and everything will have a comfortable prospect, until some desperadoes, assisted by a monster with many heads, shall start new difficulties, and put the world again into a flame; but these shall be but of short duration.

11. Before the expiration of 1725, an eagle from the north shall fly directly to the south, and perch upon the palace of a prince, and first unravel the bloody projects and designs of a wicked set of people, and then publicly discover the murder of a great king, and the intended assassination of another greater than he.

12. In 1726, three princes will be born that will grow up to be men, and inherit the crowns of three of the greatest monarchies in Europe.

13. About this time the pope will die, and after a great many intrigues and struggles, a Spanish cardinal shall be elected, who

shall decline the dignity, and declare his marriage with a great lady, heiress of one of the chief principalities in Italy, which may occasion new troubles in Europe, if not timely prevented.

14. In 1727, new troubles shall break out in the north, occasioned by the sudden death of a certain prince, and the avarice and ambition of another. Poor Poland seems to be pointed at; but the princes of the south shall enter into a confederacy to preserve her, and shall at length restore her peace, and prevent the perpetual ruin of her constitution.

15. Great endeavours will be used about this time for a comprehension in religion, supported by crafty and designing men, and a party of mistaken zealots, which they shall artfully draw in to join with them; but as the project is ill-concerted, and will be worse managed, it will come to nothing; and soon afterwards an effectual mode will be taken to prevent the like attempt for the future.

16. 1728 will be a year of inquiry and retrospection. Many exorbitant grants will be reassumed, and several persons who thought themselves secure will be called before the senate, and compelled to disgorge what they have unjustly pillaged either from the crown or the public.

17. About this time a new scaffold will be erected upon the confines of a certain great city, where an old count of a new extraction, that has been of all parties and true to none, will be doomed by his peers to make his first appearance. After this an old lady who has often been exposed to danger and disgrace, and sometimes brought to the very brink of destruction, will be brought to bed of three daughters at once, which they shall call Plenty, Peace, and Union; and these three shall live and grow up together, be the glory of their mother, and the comfort of posterity for many generations.

This is the substance of what he either writ or extracted from his papers in the interval between the loss of his speech and the return of his fit, which happened exactly at the time he had computed.

Upon the approach of his fit, he made signs to be put to bed, which was no sooner done but he was seized with extreme agonies, which he bore up under with the greatest steadfastness, and after a severe conflict, that lasted near eight hours, he expired.

Thus lived and thus died this extraordinary person; a person, though of mean extraction and obscure life, yet when his character comes to be fully and truly known, it will be read with pleasure, profit, and admiration.

His perfections at large would be the work of a volume, and inconsistent with the intention of these papers. I will, therefore, only add, for a conclusion, that he was a man of uncommon thought and judgment, and always kept his appetites and inclinations within their just limits.

His reason was strong and manly, his understanding sound and active, and his temper so easy, equal, and complaisant, that he never fell out, either with men or accidents. He bore all things with the highest affability, and computed justly upon their value and consequence, and then applied them to their proper uses.

A LETTER FROM OXFORD

Sir,

Being informed that you speedily intend to publish some memoirs relating to our dumb countryman, Dickory Cronke, I send you herewith a few lines, in the nature of an elegy, which I leave you to dispose of as you think fit. I knew and admired the man; and if I were capable, his character should be the first thing I would attempt.

Yours. &c.

AN ELEGY, IN MEMORY OF DICKORY CRONKE, THE DUMB PHILOSOPHER.

Vitiis nemo sine nascitur; optimus ille est, Qui minimus urgetur.--HORACE.

If virtuous actions emulation raise, Then this good man deserves immortal praise. When nature such extensive wisdom lent, She sure designed him for our precedent. Such great endowments in a man unknown, Declare the blessings were not all his own; But rather granted for a time to show What the wise hand of Providence can do. In him we may a bright example see Of nature, justice, and morality; A mind not subject to the frowns of fate, But calm and easy in a servile state. He always kept a guard upon his will And feared no harm because he knew no ill. A decent posture and an humble mien, In every action of his life were seen. Through all the different stages that he went, He still appeared both wise and diligent: Firm to his word, and punctual to his trust, Sagacious, frugal, arable, and just. No gainful views his bounded hopes could sway, No wanton thought led his chaste soul astray. In short, his thoughts and actions both declare, Nature designed him her philosopher; That all mankind, by his example taught, Might learn to live, and manage every thought. Oh! could my muse the wondrous subject grace, And, from his youth, his virtuous actions trace; Could I in just and equal numbers tell How well he lived, and how devoutly fell, I boldly might your strict attention claim, And bid you learn, and copy out the man.

J. P. Exeter College, August 25th, 1719. Epitaph:

The occasion of this epitaph was briefly thus:- A gentleman, who had heard much in commendation of this dumb man, going accidentally to the churchyard where he was buried, and finding his grave without a tombstone, or any manner of memorandum of his death, he pulled out his pencil, and writ as follows:-

PAUPER UBIQUE JACET.

Near to this lonely unfrequented place, Mixed with the common dust, neglected lies The man that every muse should strive to grace, And all the world should for his virtue prize. Stop, gentle passenger, and drop a tear, Truth, justice, wisdom, all lie buried here.

What, though he wants a monumental stone, The common pomp of every fool or knave, Those virtues which through all his actions shone Proclaim his worth, and praise him in the grave. His merits will a bright example give, Which shall both time and envy too outlive.

Oh, had I power but equal to my mind, A decent tomb should soon this place adorn, With this inscription: Lo, here lies confined A wondrous man, although obscurely born; A man, though dumb, yet he was nature's care, Who marked him out her own philosopher.